THEY FEED SHARKS

BY RICHARD A. PIQUETTE

◆ FriesenPress

One Printers Way
Altona, MB R0G 0B0
Canada

www.friesenpress.com

Copyright © 2022 by Richard A. Piquette
First Edition — 2022

All rights reserved.

No part of this publication may be reproduced in any form, or by any means, electronic or mechanical, including photocopying, recording, or any information browsing, storage, or retrieval system, without permission in writing from FriesenPress.

ISBN
978-1-03-915504-6 (Hardcover)
978-1-03-915503-9 (Paperback)
978-1-03-915505-3 (eBook)

1. FICTION, SCIENCE FICTION, ALIEN CONTACT

Distributed to the trade by The Ingram Book Company

TABLE OF CONTENTS

1 **AUTHOR'S GREETING**

3 **FOREWORD**

Introduction
7 **THE TRUE PART**

Chapter 1
11 **WHO INVITED THEM ANYWAY**

Chapter 2
15 **MORE QUESTIONS THAN ANSWERS**

Chapter 3
21 **TIME WELL SPENT**

Chapter 4
29 **GOOD TIMES TURNED BAD**

Chapter 5
33 **WHO ORDERED THIS NIGHTMARE**

Chapter 6
37 **FROM BAD TO WORSE**

Chapter 7
41 **TRADITION OF FRIENDS**

Chapter 8
47 **THE REALITY BEHIND THE UNBELIEVABLE**

Chapter 9
51 TIME BETTER SPENT

Chapter 10
61 DESPERATE TIMES LEAD TO DESPERATE MEASURES

Chapter 11
81 A DREAM SEQUENCE

Chapter 12
85 TAKING OUT THE TRASH

Chapter 13
91 THEY'RE NOT GOING TO BELIEVE THIS SHIT

97 CONCLUSION

99 SPECIAL THANKS

AUTHOR'S GREETING

First off, I'd like to thank you for buying my book. Secondly, if you by chance picked it up at the airport then you seriously just made my day.

My wife and I have spent many years travelling, so it goes without saying we've spent many hours in airports and sitting on airplanes.

I've bought many books at various airport bookstores over the years.

To come clean, I'm a nonfiction fan. Ninety percent of the books I read are nonfiction.

This being said,

When I first entertained the idea of writing a book, the task seemed monumental. I've never done anything of the sort before. So when I planned things out it seemed reasonable that a fictitious novelette could be the first book I wrote. Also, I had this far-out story in my head.

I often thought how cool it would be to see my book on the rack as I searched out reading material at an airport somewhere. So I stepped up my game.

So here we have it. My first book. It's short, sweet, and simple. But I hope, at the very least, it keeps you mildly entertained for your flight.

Again I'd like to thank you for choosing my book and wish you many years of happy travels.

Rick

FOREWORD

Life is a long, windy journey. We may think we designed it and that we are the commanders of our personal existence.

But it's actually a vector of coincidence. One day we may be at the pinnacle of personal achievement, then the next thrown into the lowest depths of darkness and despair without any actions of our own making.

We are but a ship in this journey and the wind is going to fill our sails and lead us in the direction of its choosing. Sometimes that may be through a storm or nightmare of epic proportions.

We never know how we'll perform in times of adversity, when darkness is set upon us.

In this event, it's only with hope and prayer that we can emerge from the other side unscathed and continue living, leaving fear or bitterness behind. Many emerge with a nightmare locked away in the vault, never allowing it spoken of again.

✦✦✦

Beau Camp was born and raised in the Bay Area on September 4, 1992. Now twenty-eight, Beau was an average American guy living an average American life.

His live-and-let-live attitude made him favorable in most people's eyes. Never one to step on anyone's toes, he'd never found himself in a confrontation of his making. This being said, he certainly wasn't someone who would allow himself to be bullied or threatened.

Those who were close to Beau, particularly his circle of friends, wouldn't have thought that under his meek demeanor was a person of such personal strength and resolve.

Beau's average life was about to enter new territory. The winds were about to blow in unexpected happiness entwined in a turn of extremely unfavourable events.

This is Beau's story.

THEY FEED SHARKS

INTRODUCTION

THE TRUE PART

San Francisco is a city on the west coast of the United States. It sits poised at the north end of the San Francisco Peninsula and includes significant stretches of the Pacific Ocean. San Francisco is a Bay City and lies nestled on the bay that shares its name. San Fran, or "the city," as locals affectionately call it, is the seventeenth most densely populated city in America, with approximately 820,000 people.

Being a coastal city, San Francisco enjoys all the benefits of a city living and breathing ocean side. Shipping, water sports, and the fishing businesses all help to bolster the ever-thriving San Fran tourist industry. San Francisco, sitting at approximately thirty-seven degrees north, may not be as popular for sun, sand, and surf as some tropical tourist destinations, but her stunning beauty and interesting history more than make up for her lack of warm waters and UV rays.

Water in the bay flows at a cool average temperature of fifty-six degrees Fahrenheit. Because of these cool waters, tourists and locals alike have for years commonly misconceived that San Francisco sits a little too far north to attract and sustain a shark population. Particularly a white shark population. In recent years, though, it has been proven that white sharks do indeed inhabit the northern Californian coast and the San Francisco Bay. In fact, it's been found that the bay is a popular breeding ground for white sharks.

All this being said, there has never been any particular historic problem with sharks. In the last couple of years, though, local news has been reporting on an increased shark activity, with the sharks becoming more brazen than usual. A video recently surfaced when a tourist happened to capture a white shark attacking a seal, breeching out of the water in an explosion of blood and gore. All this took place within forty feet of the boat landing at Alcatraz, to the horror of unsuspecting tourists and park employees.

Scientists have blamed it all on an increase in food supply for the sharks via an increase in the bay seal populations and who knows what else.

Still, there has never been a recorded shark attack on humans in the bay. Back in the day, Alcatraz used the threat of sharks as a scare tactic to ensure prisoners happily stayed put.

| THEY FEED SHARKS

Sure, San Francisco has its share of big-city problems. Crime, homelessness, violence, drugs and, recently, missing people and strange lights in the sky.

But all in all, it does its best to live and let live, its residents cohabitating by the creed of the Beatnik hippies of the sixties.

Sequoia Bill

CHAPTER 1

WHO INVITED THEM ANYWAY

Sequoia Bill Wheeler and his son Chip had been making it a habit of getting out on the water every Sunday to get in a little fishing. They loved to get out and spend a little father/son time trying their luck catching halibut. Often to help make their schedule work, they would sometimes even head out on a night fish. Realistically, the fishing always seemed a little better at night anyway. Bill is a sixty-nine-year-old retired logger who earned his nickname Sequoia while logging cedar in Northern California back in the day. His son, Chip, a forty-five-year-old business owner, lives over in Oakland. Although Chip ran his own business, raised a family of his own, and struggled to find a free moment, he always made time for his father. Chip knew how his father loved their time together fishing.

Old Bill was a crusty-looking fellow with a weathered face, long grey eyebrows, and thick tufts of grey hair growing out of each ear. Much to the chagrin of his wife Sofie, if ever ol' Bill missed his weekly barbershop visit, his nose holes would quickly start to match his ears. Bill had gained a few pounds over the years and lost the majority of his once-curly brown hair. His voice was deep and raspy, making Bill sound gruff, but he maintained a happy, cheerful manner. He always wore a green flannel buffalo check jacket, more commonly referred to as a lumber jacket. This was Bill's uniform for most of his waking hours most of the time. Everyone loved ol' Bill.

He and Sofie had been married for nearly forty-four years. Even after all those years, they still got along well. Most people knew it was due to Sofie's ability to put up with Bill's playful teasing. Whenever ol' Bill started getting on her last nerve, she'd simply tell him that Archie Bunker was on the TV and he'd quickly scurry off to the living room. Sofie would chuckle as she'd have no idea if Archie Bunker was on or not—but it worked every time to get Bill out of her hair.

It was a typical sunny, warm day out on the water just north of the Bay Bridge. That was the usual spot they headed to. Over the years, they'd had pretty good luck in this spot, but in recent years, they had been having odd occurrences with bigger fish.

"Just reel the line in, I guess," directed ol' Bill. "I think that son of a bitch is all tangled in the line."

"Well, I don't think he's taken the bait or bitten on the hook," replied Chip.

"I know he hasn't bitten on the hook, but he's got everything all frickin' twisted up."

Even before they got the hook and sinkers within 100 feet of the surface, a massive grey body broke the surface of the water just feet from the boat. The dorsal fin was a clear indication that the fish was a white shark. Not that Chip or ol' Bill needed any further evidence of it. This big fish situation had been a regular occurrence over the last year and a half. The odd thing was, the sharks never seemed to show any real interest in the easy lunch. Even a fifty-pound halibut had been pulled to the boat without any interest from the shark. The whites never took the bait or showed any interest in pulling the catch off the hook. They just seemed to come around being a nuisance, scaring away the fish, and lingering in the area when people were out there.

"I don't know what's up with these sons of bitches. I've never seen this shit in all my years, son," said Bill.

"Yeah, it's odd," replied Chip. "I could see if they were stealing our fish as the dog fish do but these Whites don't have any interest in eating. Just coming around and being assholes." Chip got the rig to the surface and pulled the hook leader and weights into the boat with a clang.

"Yup. Bait is still there," Chip said as ol' Bill looked on, bent over with his hands on his knees to reinforce his sea legs. Chip fumbled with the hook and leader that was now tangled in the net that had been lying on the floor of the boat. He then, slowly and carefully, stood up straight, looked toward the sky, put his hands on his hips, stretched his back out with a grunt of discomfort, then passed wind.

"Good heavens, son," Bill said. "You trying to make me chum those sharks?"

They shared a chuckle.

"We need to get some down riggers, Pops," said Chip. "This reeling in these hand lines from 350 feet of water is getting a little strenuous."

"Well, better you than me, son," ol' Bill said, smiling.

"Yeah, I guess," said Chip, squinting from the glaring sun. "Seriously, what do you think is up with these damn sharks?"

"I don't know, son. It's almost like they're becoming accustomed to being served up a bigger, more substantial lunch. A special flavored snack all their own."

CHAPTER 2

MORE QUESTIONS THAN ANSWERS

Paul Walker had always dreamt of visiting San Francisco on a holiday. Part of his interest in San Francisco was the infamous prison out in the bay known as Alcatraz. A million and a half others like Paul visit the National Historic Landmark each year. Paul was excited to have finally made the tip.

After a quick ferry ride across the bay from the city, you arrive on the landing pier on Alcatraz. You board the boat at Pier 33, which is located between the San Francisco Ferry Building and Fisherman's Wharf, in San Francisco.

Once on Alcatraz, Paul joined the little group of people from his boat ride to take advantage of the complimentary history tour provided by the State Park Service staff. When the twenty-minute informative greeting was over, Paul decided to fall back and tour the island at his own pace. The pier was bustling with activity. Tourists were holding hands and keeping a short leash on their excited children.

Although Alcatraz is a massively interesting attraction, its advancing state of decay also makes it a dangerous place to explore. Much of the island and prison buildings themselves are closed off to the public as repairs and renovations are an ongoing thing. The great prison walls and outbuildings of Alcatraz tower on the cliffs overhead and around the island. The guard's tower and the famous water tower are there to admire.

Back in the day, along with the prison itself, the island was graced with a beautiful Warden's Mansion, a lighthouse, a medical building, and apartments that were constructed to house the guards and other Alcatraz employees who helped make Alcatraz tick.

In 1969, years after the prison was finally closed for good, a group of Native Americans moved onto the island to occupy it and claim ownership of the land. Sometime during the occupation, the Warden's Mansion, an adjacent medical facility, and the apartments were lit on fire and burnt to the ground. The Natives were adamant that they never lit the fires and placed blame on the forces that were trying to have them removed from the island.

✦✦✦

The smell of the ocean and food vendors filled the air at the landing. A kiosk had been set up by the Park Service to rent headphones and radios for self-guided tours. The blue skies teamed with screaming gulls ready to pounce on any dropped morsel of food. The view of San Francisco and the rest of the bay from the boat pier on Alcatraz was simply amazing. Spectacular.

Paul walked to the edge of the wooden pier and looked down into the dark Pacific water. He wanted to kill a couple of minutes to allow the others to get comfortably ahead of him. As he looked down, he noticed what appeared to be a garment floating in the water. Upon closer inspection, he saw it appeared to be a white jersey with red stripes. He could see a black number six and a name on an embroidered patch that said "Scully" printed in black. Paul didn't make it a habit of pulling trash from the ocean, but the name Scully struck his interest. Paul jumped down from the top tier onto the boat landing level just off the water. He got down on his knees and stretched out, trying to grab the fabric. With arms and neck stretched out like a chicken, he noticed his reflection in the black water and shot himself a wink and a cheesy grin. But his prize was just beyond his grasp. He jumped back to his feet to have a quick look around to see if there was something he could use to extend his reach.

Standing behind him several feet back was another Park Service employee holding a trash-picking stick, the kind with the lever-controlled claw. The fellow had a big, thick moustache that crossed his face neatly and was trimmed straight across at the bottom like a shop broom. The fellow was standing back, watching Paul.

Just as Paul was going to ask him if he could commandeer his device, the fellow walked over, offering his assistance.

Taking one knee, he said, "I think I got the required reach to just grab... and voilà. Is this what you were after?" He held the soaked item out in front of himself. He grimaced as he noticed the soaking garment was draining water on his boots.

"Ah, your clothing, I presume?" offered the park worker.

"Ah, yes. I mean no. It's not mine. I just saw it floating there and..."

The number on the garment was sixty-six. On the front were the words, "The Modesto Beer Hogs."

"Wow! This is someone's ball jersey. This is an official polyester ball jersey by Nike," Paul said, with excitement in his voice. "These things aren't cheap. This must have gotten away from someone somewhere. Why would someone just allow their team jersey to float off in the waves? Maybe someone drowned.

"Joel." Paul read the name tag on the Park Service employee's uniform.

"Who knows, these days?" replied Joel. "We've been finding all kinds of odd personal effects floating in the bay recently. It's a dumping ground. A regular boutique.

"A couple of months ago they found a woman's handbag with her ID, driver's license, credit cards, birth control, the whole nine yards. The police had tried to contact the woman but she had been reported missing by her family weeks earlier. I've heard the FBI has been involved in investigating the ever-growing list of missing people," Joel said.

"That's odd. I haven't heard anything about this on the TV," said Paul.

"Well, San Fran is a tourist city. People going missing isn't something they'd want to advertise," replied Joel.

"Oh, sounds like San Francisco may have a serial killer on their hands, Joel," Paul said. "We had a serial killer."

Joel looked into Paul's eyes as he fished for the stranger's name and waited.

"Oh. Paul. My name is Paul."

"Remember the Zodiac Killer, Paul?" Joel said. "He was ours."

"Oh, yeah. Right. Well, maybe you have sharks," Paul said jokingly.

"We have sharks also, Paul. Oh, we have sharks."

Joel Reber had worked for the San Francisco Park Service on Alcatraz for sixteen years. His duties varied from tour guide to security to even minor repairs. From time to time, he would even help out in the Alcatraz store. Everybody liked old Joel, but it was common knowledge that he wasn't very good with money and figuring out customers' change from their purchases. The girls in the store did their best to ensure he didn't operate the till, and not to hurt his feelings. Still, they liked it when the books jived at the end of the day.

Joel certainly knew his way around and was well versed in the island's history. He was known for being friendly and helpful. The Park Service knew he was kind of lazy, but was happy to just have ol' Joel and his big moustache wandering around, being the friendly guy he was.

To make extra money he would regularly work the night shift doing security. From time to time, people would boat out at night and try to get on the island and hide out. This was unwise, not to mention extremely dangerous, and the Park Service took trespassing seriously. Also, much of the repair and renovation work was carried out at night. Alcatraz was always a busy place, twenty-four-seven.

CHAPTER 3

TIME WELL SPENT

Considering how lonely I've been for the past year, it was nice to be out. "On a date." OK, there, I said it. *A date*.

Spending time with Vicki tonight was turning out to be nice. Definitely what I needed. I thought we'd have dinner at Scona's On The Pier. Scona's is an old favorite eatery of mine. My mom started taking me there for fish and chips when I was a kid and I had been going there for special occasions ever since.

Vicki had a salmon dish with edamame beans and I had the Oysters Rockefeller and risotto. I always had the Oysters Rockefeller and risotto at Scona's. It was my fave. Strangely, I was still a little hungry after my main course but I left it at that and didn't order any dessert. I didn't want to come across as being a hog on our first date together. Vicki bravely tackled the Mud Pie though. She offered to share, but I declined the offer.

Mud Pie is a chocolaty coffee ice cream infused with crumbled Oreo bits and covered with a thin chocolate shell. I sat there very nonchalantly as she worked her way through it. I did my best not to let on that I was coveting her dessert. She was unaware that if she wasn't there I would have devoured it and whatever fingers got in the way, like a starving lion.

We washed our meal down with a bottle of wine. Neither of us are big drinkers as was apparent when we foolishly ordered a red wine. The server was kind enough to inform us that a white wine generally went better with fish.

"Oh, OK, I see." Vicki and I sat there looking up at him for direction. "Then what would you recommend?" I asked.

"Well, sir, the sauvignon blanc is very popular," the server said.

"Savvy blan, wow, sounds exquisite," I said with a chuckle. Vicki looked at me and smiled. She got what I did there. The server just stood there with his pen and paper at the ready but gave no indication that he found me amusing.

"Ah, yes, OK, that sounds great. We'll give that a try," I said.

Wine seemed to be the thing people did on a date these days. I thought, though, who was I to say, really? Mr. "First Date in Two Years" guy.

After dinner, we rushed outside so Vicki could fire up a smoke. She led the way. Vicki reached into her left back jeans pocket and pulled out a pack of Newports and a blue Bic lighter. She carried her wallet in her front right pocket.

She had her pack open, a smoke in her mouth and lit before I even realized it. She motioned the open pack in my direction as an offering.

Awkwardly, I said, "Ah, no thank you. I've been trying to cut back to only several dozen a day." Vicki's face lit up with a smile, as we both knew I didn't smoke.

After dinner, we walked up Jefferson Street, past the big Fisherman's Wharf sign and stopped briefly to listen to the GroWiser Band, which often situated themselves at the sign. There was a Black dude dressed in a funky seventies disco-looking outfit dancing away. He and the band were pretty good so we watched till they were done. Then we continued on to the Embarcadero. As we walked along, I happened to see a cool little blue handbag hanging on a rack of bags in the doorway of a shop. I told Vicki, "Wait here for one second. I'll be right back."

"What? what are you doing? Where are you going?" Vicki asked.

"Just wait here—I'll only be a minute," I replied.

As I promised, I was back in but a minute, concealing something behind my back.

"What do you got there, Beau?" Vicki asked, trying to look around me. "What do you got?" She reached behind me from the right then the left.

"Ah, I got you a little present," I said. "Oh my God! What did you get me?" Vicki said, excitedly jumping up and down.

"Ah, oh, it's nothing, really, I just thought you could use a..."

"Oh my God! A handbag!" Vicki shrieked as I handed it to her. "Oh my God, I love it. I love it, it's beautiful. Thank you so much. It's beautiful."

"Well, I thought you could use something to carry your things around in."

She quickly put her wallet, smokes, lighter, and something she'd dug out of her left front pocket into her new bag. Flung it over her shoulder and began to strike numerous handbag modelling poses as she giggled. I thought it was the cutest thing I'd ever seen. She hugged me and kissed me on the cheek.

I thought to myself, *Jeez, I gotta buy her more things*.

Vicki grabbed my hand as we continued along the Embarcadero, passing Pier 39, another San Francisco tourist hot spot.

Pier 39 is just that, a pier, But it's basically a shopping center with restaurants, shops, video arcades, food stands, and kids' rides. The Aquarium Of The Bay is on the pier, as well. In my opinion, the best part is along the northwest end of the pier. Over the edge of the pier and off into the water they built floating piers for seals and sea lions. The floating piers usually have no vacancy, as they're more often than not totally covered with the pudgy critters, sprawled out and relaxing in the sun. Sometimes they make quite a racket barking and carrying on. There is always a tourist that has to bark at them and get them going. The tourists think they're smart getting the critters to bark but I'm pretty sure it's the other way around. But it's amusing to watch nonetheless.

I asked Vicki if she wanted to check it out. "Another time," she said, smiling. "Let's just walk and talk."

"Sounds good to me, Vicki," I said. We kept walking along the Embarcadero to the Skygate. We stopped and listened to a couple of street performers before continuing. Then crossed the road and turned right onto Kearny Street.

"Have you ever been up to Coit Tower?" Vicki asked.

"Yes, I have. I hang out there from time to time."

"Let's go up there," she said excitedly.

"Well, OK. I think it's closed, but . . ." Before I could finish, she said, "That's OK. Let's go up."

As we headed up Kearny and away from Fisherman's Wharf, there was less traffic. It got quieter and quieter as we left the bay behind.

I guess I hadn't given it a lot of thought. I'd never made my way from the Embarcadero up Kearny toward Coit Tower. I always elected to drive and get there and approach on my Vespa or Ross's Vega, via Telegraph Road.

It's a bit of a lofty endeavour from the Embarcadero as it meanders its way through short back streets till you find yourself at the base of Telegraph Hill. Then you have the Filbert Steps to deal with. The Filbert Steps are a set of 600 wooden and concrete pedestrian steps that make their way up Telegraph Hill and come out in the parking lot near the base of the tower. You gain an elevation of 230 feet.

We walked arm in arm till we got to the steps, then I allowed Vicki to take the lead. The Filbert Steps are famous for the flowers, architecture of the houses, and view of the bay. To be honest, the only view I was interested in was Vicki's Levis as she climbed the steps ahead of me.

As we made our way up, I stopped to point out various flowers and birds and things. I tried not to make it too obvious that what I was doing was catching my breath. I think Vicki was onto me. But Vicki was more than happy smelling every flower I pointed out. As we journeyed up, lights were coming on all across the city and the bay. It's hard to describe how beautiful San Francisco Bay is as the sun starts to go down.

Turned out it was a great idea to venture up there. The little journey had taken us a while, so as we got to the top, it was starting to get dark. We made our way over to the tower, but, as I had suspected, it was closed and locked up. The parking lot was empty. Everyone had left. Usually, there was the odd vehicle there after dark as the teenagers liked to come up here to park and make out.

Sounded reasonable to me.

"Well, what do you think, Vick? Should we check out the park before we figure out how we're going to get down from here?" I asked. "Or should we scram before it gets really dark?"

"You're not scared of the dark, are you, Beauy?" Vicki said as she grabbed my hand, making a pouty face.

"Ah. No. I just wouldn't want my girlfriend to poke out an eye on a branch or something on our first date," I replied.

"Am I your girlfriend?" Vicki said playfully.

I'm glad it was a little too dark out for Vicki to see my face turn red.

I thought to myself: *Open mouth, insert foot.*

It was quiet in the park. The sky was clear. The stars were out. The last of the sun had fallen into the ocean. Most of what little light there was came from the rising moon. It was a splendid evening. There is nothing like an autumn full moon in central California. I had often found myself here in the park at the foot of the tower throughout the past year. I enjoyed coming there, but I would always come alone and usually during the day. I'd think to myself how nice it would be to be there with someone special, but I also enjoyed my quiet time. Now there I was with a certain someone. My dreams were coming true.

We walked down a cobblestone trail lit by small ornamental streetlights that had posts fashioned with greenish patina-covered gargoyles. The foliage smelled wonderful as the timer-set sprinklers came on randomly and dampened the leaves. We continued past the outdoor swimming pool, which had been barren of water since early September. I thought we could sit on the edge of the empty pool for a while but the gate was locked.

We found ourselves sitting on a seesaw in the kiddie park area. I sat with my feet on the ground as Vicki sat suspended above me, looking down and hanging onto the metal handle with one hand. With her other hand, she playfully held her new handbag up over in my direction, saying, "Look what I have" as she giggled. Vicki looked beautiful there in the moonlight. She spoke so softly but I could hear every word she said. I could hear her breathe. Vicki had one of those smiles that never seemed to leave her face. I think we were both truly enjoying each other's company and I think a romance was blossoming.

The dream was about to end.

CHAPTER 4

GOOD TIMES TURNED BAD

Although we were in the tourist area of the city, I surmised that we hadn't seen anyone for well over an hour. Mind you, it was getting late, I suppose. San Francisco is a relatively safe city considering her size and Vicki and I were so caught up in each other that we hadn't noticed our solitude. I could hear a dog bark and the odd car horn from down the hill along the Embarcadero. It was so quiet we could hold a very soft conversation.

We got ready to make our way back down the hill to grab a coffee somewhere along Jefferson.

"Are you ready to head down, Vicki?" I asked.

"Not really. It's so quiet and calm up here. But I suppose we should.... Or maybe you can think of another activity before we go down," Vicki said playfully as she chewed on her index finger.

"Ah, well, let me see here," I said, mimicking her finger chewing as I look up to the sky in thought.

"Hey, that's odd," I said. Look how there is a great big area right above us where the stars have vanished. I wonder how that..."

Suddenly, without any warning, a blinding white light and deafening mechanical buzzing noise washed over us from above. I could feel a strong pulse of static electricity as my hair stood on end and I smelled burnt ozone. It so startled us that Vicki screamed and fell backward off the seesaw, crashing to the ground and ending up belly down in the dirt where the grass had been worn away by playing kids. I rolled off my seat onto the ground to my left. As I got to my knees, I could see Vicki running off into the trees toward Pioneer Pool. Her new bag was still draped over her shoulder. The light was so bright I couldn't turn my eyes to the sky.

I took chase after her with one hand shielding my eyes from the light. My dirty hand flung dirt into my eyes. I tripped and fell again before I reached the tree line where I'd last seen her. My knee painfully popped as I got back to my feet and sprinted into the canopy of Monterey Cypress. As I entered the trees, my eyes were briefly relieved from the blinding light but my pupils took a couple of seconds to adjust. I tried to get the dust out of my eyes by pulling my top lashes but my hands were filthy and it wasn't working. My heart was pounding and I was having trouble catching my breath. I stopped and called out to Vicki, but there was no sign of her.

Before I could even start running again, the bright light that was once overhead was now on the ground and just behind me and coming into the trees. Now the trees that were in front of the light between it and myself cast bizarre dancing shadows ahead of me as the light moved. The light was so bright it made the trees look like thin black threads. The buzz seemed to be emanating from the light. It moved in tune with the position of the light. I barrelled forward through the trees. Out of control, I dodged tree after tree. To say it was "a turkey shoot," is an understatement. I had no idea what was in front of me. Every time I glanced back, my pupils would shrink and I would be completely blinded again.

The noise now was so loud it caused a ringing in my ears. Surely someone else nearby could hear this. I ran with my hands cupped over my ears. The light was seconds behind me. I could feel the radiant heat from the light. I ran unintentionally through what I guess was an opening in a chain-link fence. A strand of wire tore at my face. I fell across a flat concrete area, got back to my feet, took two steps, then plunged into the abyss.

All went black.

CHAPTER 5

WHO ORDERED THIS NIGHTMARE

I'd never been so cold in my life. But I could still tell that I had been lying on something extremely hard. Not only was I cold—I was in complete utter darkness, except for what I had perceived as a small white LED light above and off to my right. It strangely emitted no illumination as its light waves were completely absorbed by the darkness. I stared at it intensely as there was nothing else before me for my eyes to fix themselves to. I tried to gather my thoughts, my memory. *What the fuck was this?* None of it was there. I needed to get a grip of myself.

My arms were at my sides as I could feel the cold skin from my upper thighs on my fingertips. I could tell by the way the cold seared my skin on my back and butt that I was lying against a hard, extremely cold surface—I think maybe ice or something. I ran my frozen fingertips slowly along the surface beside me. It had a texture, a grain. Like granite or something. I lifted my head and clunked it back down a couple of times to verify the hardness of the slab.

There was a sound emanating from somewhere. A hum. It seemed to encompass the entire space. It made my ears tingle and itchy as it vibrated through the table into the back of my skull. Still, I could hear my heart beating in my ears.

Although I was freezing my ass off, the humming sound was somehow soothing. Along with the hum, there was an odour. A strangely odd but familiar odour. It reminded me of that smell you get when cutting through bone or hoof material or de-horning farm animals. I know that's a strange statement. But that's what I'd liken it to. Maybe not quite that strong. Kind of a residual lingering stench.

When I was young, I spent time at my Uncle John and Aunt Elma's farm up in Canada. John was my mom's brother. My mom and dad would haul me up north to visit them every summer until I was at least thirteen. We never went there in the winter. Even though there were years my mom wanted us to head up for Christmas, my dad would refuse. Claiming it was 900 below and there was no way he was going to Canada in the winter. But then again, dad also said the mosquitos in Canada were the size of pigeons. I personally never witnessed that. It was many years later that

I learned that it never actually quite got down to 900 below in Canada.

My uncle raised cows, chickens, and pigs, and had a couple of horses. I always brought my cowboy hat and immediately became a rancher/cowboy while I was there. It was my favourite thing in the world. I always hated to have to go home after being a cowboy for a week. One year, my uncle surprised me with my very own pair of Boulet cowboy boots. They weren't new, but that was OK. I think Boulet boots are proudly Canadian or something like that. I still have them to this day. Although they don't fit. They still have dried cow shit on them. Strangely, I loved the smell of cow shit. That cow shit on those boots is one of my prized childhood possessions. Even today I keep them in a boot tray right at my front door for all to see and to shock my yuppie San Francisco friends with my tough cowboy upbringing. They'd say, "Wow! Did you work on a ranch? Do you break horses and stuff?" I'd lie and say, "Yeah, of course. I broke hundreds of horses."

When we drove home from uncle's farm, Dad would wrap my boots in three layers of garbage bags and wouldn't allow them in the front of the car.

During my cowboy life, my uncle and I did it all while my dad hid in the house with the ladies. My dad was a military man, but he had no stomach for getting dirty. Or animals. Or smell. Or shit and stuff.

We branded cows, we de-horned bulls. We trimmed hooves and shoed horses. We even cut the prairie oysters off the male cows. Uncle John fed those prairie oysters to my dad for years and he was never the wiser. He just thought they were the best baseball steaks he ever ate. Uncle Johnny said we'd keep that little secret under our hats and that cowboys never repeated something once it was under a hat.

My Uncle John was my favourite uncle and his farm was my all-time favourite place in the world. One time I told him the only way his farm could be any better was if it were near the ocean.

My Uncle John was a certified landlubber. "Nothing good ever came out of the ocean," Uncle John would say. "Remember that, Beau. Nothing good ever came out of the ocean."

CHAPTER 6

FROM BAD TO WORSE

It's funny how, when you lie in complete darkness, you can't get a handle on time. I'm not sure how long I had been lying there since I had woken up. Several minutes, maybe. I had slowly started to regain my wits about me though. I had contemplated swinging my legs out and maybe standing up. I didn't even know whether there was a floor beneath me. So I was hesitant to do so. My cheek was stinging and my ass was numb from the cold.

Suddenly, the bone odour became stronger. Damn well pungent. It seemed to come and go as if carried by a breeze that didn't exist. The hum pulsated. I thought I could hear shuffling in the darkness around my position. I was sensing a presence. My fright-or-flight response was definitely firing on all cylinders. I wanted to bolt, but I was too frightened to move. Literally scared shitless. Can you picture a 179-pound dude being frozen with fear? That was me at that moment. But when I get scared—I mean really scared—I get mad. I think it's a coping mechanism. I could feel anger creating a welcome heat in my face. I have a habit of doing stupid shit when I get angry and I was sensing things were about to become stupid.

Suddenly, Vicki popped into my mind, which momentarily grounded my thoughts. Oh my God. Where was Vicki? "Vicki?" I whispered loudly. "Vicki?"

I may have been intensely cold, but suddenly I felt something brush against my foot in the darkness. Now whether there was a floor or no floor beneath me I was going to stand the fuck up.

I guess it was a leap of faith, but I swung my legs out and sprang to my feet. Something sharp ripped at the back of my leg as I slid from the table. There seemed to be a scurrying sound around me in the darkness, as if maybe I'd startled something. I stopped and stayed still.

Hold still for a second, I thought to myself. *Listen.* The surface beneath my feet was cold as ice. I reached back to feel a burning on the back of my leg. It was warm and sticky. Pretty sure I was bleeding. And to my further surprise, I was butt-ass naked.

My eyes were beginning to adjust to the darkness, or, the room was beginning to get brighter. One or the other. It was like the area was on a dimmer switch with someone very slowly turning up the lights. I looked over to where

I thought the little LED light was situated to help regain my bearings. It looked the same as before but it flashed as if something passed between it and me. I pointed my eyes ahead. There was something. Something just several feet in front of me.

"Hello? Is someone there"? "I can see you," I said. There was no response but now I heard shuffling behind me and to my right.

I was surrounded.

"Look, guys. I'm 'bout to lose my shit here. I ain't fucking around," I said bravely.

CHAPTER 7

TRADITION OF FRIENDS

On Fridays after work, we had made it a tradition to head to the beach. Ross and I, usually because of traffic, had to park the Vega a couple of blocks up and walk down to the water. We lived a couple of doors from each other, about two miles from our favorite beach hangout bay side. The beach was pretty much downhill from where we lived. That means at the end of the day it would have been a two-mile hike up the hill if we had decided to walk it. It wasn't a big deal, but if you are familiar with the city, you'd understand the issue with that. San Francisco has some challenging hills, to say the least. So we always drove the hilly section. I'd been telling Ross we should start taking the trolley.

"Why should we take the trolley when we have the beast?" Ross would say. I kept telling him that one of these days we'd be pushing the beast up the hill. He'd do a double finger point at me, wink, and say, "Good one, Maynard."

Parking a couple of blocks up was OK with Ross and me because we had made it a routine of stopping by the Ghirardelli Chocolate Factory. They had a small storefront in the Ghirardelli Square building along the way on Larkin Street, just across Beach Street from the Beach Park. The Ghirardelli building encompassed the entire city block, from Beach Street to North Point and Polk to Larkin Street. The Ghirardelli building at one time was a wool factory but had been bought and operated by Ghirardelli since 1852. Today the building is home to some forty shops and vendors.

Every Friday as we headed to the beach, I'd always buy Macy a treat. Pretty sure chocolate was Macy's favourite thing in the world. Macy had explained how her grandmother was of French origin and would pronounce chocolate as *shocola*. So, naturally, Macy would always say *shocola*. It was so cute watching her become childlike before my eyes every time she was given chocolate. She'd stuff a handful in her mouth. Then her eyes would roll up to the sky and she'd bend at the knees as if her legs were buckling. It became a regular performance. Made us laugh every time.

On this day, Ross insisted on buying the *shocola*, so I just waited outside. How could anyone go in there and not fill their face with chocolate?

"OK, I'll be back in a second," said Ross. "Wait here."

"Where am I going to go, Maynard?" I replied.

As I waited, I noticed the red newspaper box situated on the curb. I wandered over in its general direction. My original intentions were to lean on it. To be honest, I've never bought a newspaper in my life. Inside the box's little plastic window I saw a rather colorful front cover that caught my eye. It was an issue of the city's favourite newspaper, The *San Francisco Chronicle*. I crouched over with my hands on my knees trying to see through the weathered plastic window. In bold black print, the headline on the front cover read: "More Unexplained Lights over San Francisco. Witnessed by Hundreds." The headline sat over a half-page colored photo of the Bay Bridge. A smaller story inserted on the cover simply read, in the form of a question, "Aliens in Mir Woods?"

I chuckled. The ol' *Chronicle* must be having trouble selling papers these days. I thought of grabbing that paper but I didn't have the right change. I pulled at the edges of the plastic window and the little door with the possibility of scoring a free paper.

"Hey, what are you doing?" said a voice behind me. I could see Ross's reflection over my shoulder in the plexiglass news box window.

"Hey, did you see this?" I attempted to reply.

"What now? You're reading? What next, Maynard?" Ross said, cutting me off. "Let's go. Chocolate's getting expensive, brah. Did you know they sell chocolate-covered coffee beans in there? That shit's good. They gave me some to try. It's roasted coffee beans covered in chocolate. Did I mention they gave me some? I had a handful."

"I would have never guessed, Maynard," I told him as I rolled my eyes. We continued down the hill toward the beach.

Macy took the trolley from where she lived in the Presidio. It came to the Hyde and Beach public transit kiosk just east of the beach park.

We'd go down and hang out on the beach-front bleachers and watch the girls and the swimmers swimming laps in the freezing water along the wave-breaker. That's where the San Francisco Bay Open Water Swim Club would practice. Those crazy bastards would swim the two miles several times a year from the San Fran Harbor Pier across to Alcatraz. I'd always wondered how many of them had gotten eaten by sharks over the years. It's not like they'd tell anyone that, if one of the participants vanished, it wouldn't be good for business or tourism to have people eaten by big fish. The San Francisco Bay has one of the biggest white shark breeding areas along the Pacific West Coast. Nobody seems to know that, but it is apparently a fact.

We love to hang out at the beach. We don't really do much. Just kind of loiter around and take in the sun. Personally, I'm not much for swimming. I'm a strong swimmer, but I've always found the water too cold here in the northwest. I'm happy up here onshore being a beach troll, as Macy calls us.

Ross, on the other hand, loves the water.

On this day, Macy had brought the beer. That's what happens when you lose a bet at work. You bring the beer on Friday. And it's not an easy task to get booze into the beach park. You have to find an ingenious way to smuggle it by the snoopy beach cops. They're always on the make for people trying to bring alcohol on the beach. They don't allow alcohol on the beach, although once you claim your little area of turf, whether it is in the stands or on the sand, they don't seem to worry about the rule anymore. San Francisco By-Law Ordinance 227-4. Yet in the city, everyone and their dog are stoned out of their minds on who knows what. That's part of San Francisco's DNA, back from her Beatnik grandparents. Everyone smokes the weed.

To my surprise, not only did Macy bring the Coors on this day, but she also brought her friend. A cute, freckle-faced redhead with blue eyes and a great smile named Vicki.

This was going to be a good day, I thought to myself.

CHAPTER 8

THE REALITY BEHIND THE UNBELIEVABLE

As I stood there, nude in the darkness, the room took another turn to become brighter. As the cloak of darkness lifted, the mystery of what was going on around me was now out of the bag and things were only getting shittier by the minute.

Standing there with my mouth open and my pecker out, I could now somewhat make out what stood before me. There were two small, skinny creatures standing just to the right of the table at the end. Fricken alien things, I swear to you. I'm guessing four feet tall. Their heads weren't as high as the table I had just jumped off. They weren't grey, as the stories go, but a tannish, brownish color.

"What–the–fuck?" I may have muttered out loud.

The room continued to slowly brighten up.

These things were standing motionless close together, although they seemed to shuffle. Like when people ride a packed subway car. They stood there with their scrawny arms at their sides looking at me. The little bastards' heads were large with very small black eyes like a catfish. They were identical in appearance. Their faces were flat and expressionless other than wrinkles and grooves in the orbital area that gave them the appearance they were stern or angry at me. There was a straight slit that ran across the lower face that I'm guessing was a mouth. In the middle of the face were two small round holes that looked like nostrils. Their chins moulded into skinny necks.

I gazed at them intensely. As the room lightened, my vision sharpened. It looked like the front of the throat was a separate tube from the spine. One in front of the other. It appeared to separate from the neck just under the head then came down to connect to the upper chest at the top where the sternum is. It was transparent and I strained to see if anything moved in it. I had never seen anything like that in my life.

There were no other facial features or anything that looked like ears or hair. They didn't appear to be wearing any type of clothing and there were no indications of gender that I bothered to look for. Their bodies and legs were scrawny but looked stripped in muscular sinews. I could see bluish veins through the skin.

There were two of the midgets directly in front of me and two more off slightly to my right. I slowly cranked my neck as far as I could in their direction. I could see another one behind me. Then I looked to my left. My peripheral vision was working overtime. I watched for shit to move. I expected something to jump out at me. I didn't trust that fucker standing behind me. A shiver ran through my body as I could feel my hair stand up on my arms. There was so much to take in and I felt so vulnerable standing there naked and cold.

We stood there looking at each other. I expected them to move. For some reason, I expected them to talk or make a gesture or something.

"You fuckers brought me here. What do you want?" I said.

But they just stood there with that pissed look on their faces. The aliens to my right seemed to be slowly floating toward the other two near the table. The light near the floor was still poor so I couldn't see their lower legs or feet. The odd movement freaked me out.

Just behind the two freaks that stood in front of me were these two tall, lanky black things. I'm guessing seven feet tall. Everything was so black they only started to come into view as the room got even brighter. They also had these long necks that hung over, draping forward like a buzzard. I didn't know if these things were alive or some sort of statue.

I must be dreaming. This can't be real, I thought in disbelief. *Did I hit my head? Wasn't I in the park? Where was Vicki?*

I needed to get a grip. Fast.

RICHARD A. PIQUETTE |

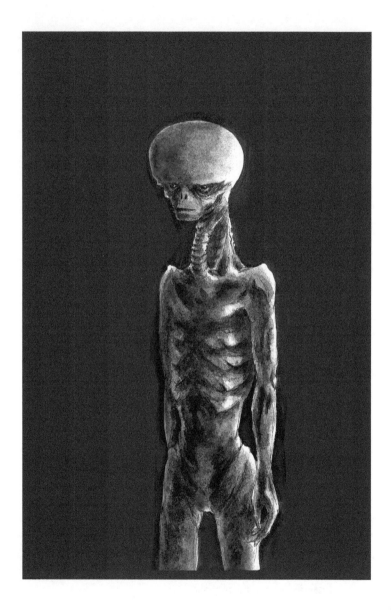

CHAPTER 9

TIME BETTER SPENT

The nice thing about mid-California is you can still hang around on the beach in October and not freeze your ass off. On a nice day, you'll still see a brave young lady or two wearing a bikini.

The bleachers at the Aquatic Park were concrete. They were built back in the sixties, around the time they built the wave-breaker wall. The wave-breaker wall is part of the Aquatic Park Cove Municipal Pier. The whole thing is about 450 feet long and curves off in a paisley shape toward the east. Toward Fisherman's Wharf. The pier is also concrete. If you look down over the edge, you'll see a large build-up of seaweed and stones along its length that vanish into the blue depths. When you get to the end of the pier, there is a large square concrete structure about eight feet by eight feet by six and a half feet high that at one time had a statue or monument or something on its top. The statue is no longer there. The pier, although run down, is safe and still offers a great view of the city from the water and serves its purpose of creating a calm safe area for the swimmers.

Ross Weber is my best friend. We also work together in the mechanical department at the university. Ross, Macy, and I have been best buds since grade school. We grew up living on the same block just off the Presidio. Our fathers worked for the navy and were stationed in San Fran. They worked at the Naval Air Station Alameda, just over the bridge in Oakland. They carpooled to work every day. Our parents were friends and our families were close. Our mothers were homemakers and best friends who spent every day together so there was no question that Macy, Ross, and I would be beasties.

The three of us went to the same high school. Galileo High.

Hey, our high school was famous. Or maybe I should say infamous. Galileo High School is where OJ Simpson learned to play football.

Yup, *that* OJ Simpson.

He went on to make a name for himself. In more ways than one.

There was a time when our school was immensely proud of OJ.

When we were attending school there they had an entire display case set up to honor him right at the front door. You literally couldn't get in the building without being informed that Galileo was the home of OJ Simpson. They had jerseys, ribbons, trophies, pictures, you name it. Even a picture of OJ and the mayor.

All that stuff has long since been removed since OJ's fall from grace.

Galileo High School is now called the Galileo Academy of Science and Technology.

Macy went on to attend the UOSF, where she got her masters in business. She got offered a job there just after she graduated. She's a smart girl. To be honest, Macy got Ross and me our jobs there.

Macy is a pretty girl. She's tall with dark brown hair and a nice figure. She has big brown eyes and a perfect complexion. The guys were always hitting on her, growing up. They still do. I used to get so mad. Not because I thought Macy should be my girlfriend. It was more that I always tried to protect her. More like a sister/brother thing. One time, I punched a guy in the nose. He wasn't even being an asshole or anything. After that episode, Macy took me aside and read me the riot act. I've since become more respectful, although I'm still protective.

Along with Ross, Macy is my best friend, as well. I love her more than anything in the world.

Ross, on the other hand, is a real ham. We always bring Ross with us every chance we can because he's always guaranteed to say or do something silly and, hey, as I mentioned, he's my best bud.

On this day we were sitting at the beach two beers down each, and he up and proclaimed, "It's turned out to be a super nice day. I'm glad I wore my swimsuit." He stood up and slid his sweatpants off to reveal a rather risqué lime green Speedo with a frog's face on the crotch. Macy spit out a mouthful of beer. Most of which ended up on my lap. Then he pulled his Chip and Pepper T-shirt off. He did it in a way that you'd see a woman do it—seductively. Afterward, he waved his hair freely about as if in the breeze, though he actually has no hair to wave. He keeps his cut pretty much down to the wood.

To our surprise, he had on his sister's bikini top. Ross's sister Tulip is a fairly well-endowed young lady with double Ds. She lives with Ross but how he got that bra I don't know. She'd be pissed if she knew her brother was borrowing her clothes for comic relief. Ross has a chest like an eight-year-old. Zero pecs, so the cups of the top hung flat, down toward his gut. We all laughed our asses off as he proclaimed he had to use the washroom and commenced to step down the bleacher to the sand. Then he walked toward the water, wiggling his ass as everyone on the beach watched in horror. I almost pissed myself laughing. I was sure he was going to get his ass kicked.

I looked at Vicki. I don't think she got the humor. I told her not to worry about Ross. "He's kind of retarded," I said. She looked at me and gave me a little smile. "He's funny," she said.

"What's at the end of that pier thing?" she asked.

"Not much," I answered. "Just a block of concrete. Ah, would you like to see it?"

With a little smile, she said, "Sure."

I asked Macy if she wanted to come. "No, I'll wait here for Kermit," she replied.

"OK, we'll be back in a flash then," I said.

It was a fantastic day. The sun was bright. The temperature was seventy-one degrees and the water inside the protected cove area was calm. People were out swimming around, braving the cold water. Vicki and I walked down the pier as I pointed out various interesting things around the bay. We approached two hippy dudes who were standing around smoking weed. It was sort of funny as they were engulfed in a cloud of smoke that didn't seem to want to disperse as there was no wind to carry it away. We eased over to the other side of the pier, not wanting to disturb their little atmosphere. We made our way to the end of the pier, where I hoisted Vicki up on the top of the concrete structure. She jumped to her feet, looked around, and said, "Hey. This is great up here. I can see everything. There's the Golden Gate."

There were bolts still in the side for the concrete where a plaque once was fastened. So I tried to hook my sneaker on them to get up beside her. Luckily some other guy was there who helped me up. Vicki dug a pack of smokes out from her back pocket.

"Hey. Do you have a light?" Vicki asked the guy.

"Ah, yeah I do," he replied. His girlfriend dug a blue Bic lighter out of her purse and handed it to him. He then passed it up with a little toss. "And you can keep that one," The guy told her.

"Oh my God, thanks," Vicki said, smiling.

"No problem," he said as he and his girlfriend turned and walked down the pier toward land. As they reached the shore they stepped off the concrete onto the sand then started following the shoreline toward Fisherman's Wharf. They gave us a little wave and we waved back.

Vicki Doss was new to San Fran. She started college at the University of San Francisco just months ago—enrolled in the MSN nursing program. I thought she must be from a family with money as that program cost $32,000. Vicki was a farm girl from Murdo, South Dakota. Murdo is a small farming community sitting out along I-90, about 137 miles east of Rapid City. Vicki attended the Jones County High School in Murdo, where she was class valedictorian her senior year. Her father owned a ranch near Murdo and her mother worked as a nurse at the Jones County Medical Clinic. Vicki grew up on the ranch, helping to raise the animals. A true farm girl.

She was happy to be taking her schooling here on the coast. She had never seen the ocean until she had moved here. She certainly fit right in with her freckles and lovely Southern California look.

Macy works at the UOSF in the university's administration department. That's where she and Vicki met. Macy helped get Vicki enrolled and situated for her first year. They hit it off immediately and hung together all week.

Again, I also work there as does Ross, but hadn't until today been introduced to Vicki. Macy had been holding out on me.

Vicki and I hit it off well. I told her about my time spent on my uncle's ranch up in Canada and tried to make it sound like I was some kind of cowboy and how I was sent for every year to help with the ranching duties. OK, I may have embellished a little. She probably was thinking that I was a real doofus but she smiled and laughed at everything I said. At one point we talked about cows, I tried to tell her about feeding the prairie oysters to my dad but I said cow oysters. She corrected me and said prairie oysters. "We call them prairie oysters back home," she said.

"Ah, yeah. Prairie oysters. What did I say?"

"You said cow oysters," Vicki said with a giggle. "But I know what you mean." I could feel my face turn warm and red.

Vicki talked a lot about the farm, animals, and nursing. I could tell she was a smart girl. I thought that I might be out of my league with this one but she was very attentive and made me feel like I was interesting and funny.

At some point, Vicki ended up holding my hand. We sat there and talked for about an hour until Macy and Ross came along and told us it was time to go.

"We thought maybe you guys fell in the ocean or something," Macy said, smiling.

I said, "Oh, are you guys still here?"

Vicki laughed.

We gathered our things, threw our empty Coors cans in the trash can at the bottom of the bleachers, and made our way up to the trolley kiosk.

"OK, well, I guess we'll see you guys later then," I said. I turned and looked at Vicki. "So we're going to meet at the Fisherman's Wharf sign at four tomorrow then?"

"OK, I can't wait. I'll see you then," Vicki replied, smiling.

"Well OK then," we all said at the same time.

We stood there in an awkward moment of silence, all kind of looking at one another, not knowing what to do next. So I rigidly stepped forward and kissed Macy on the cheek, then turned and kissed Vicki on the cheek. Macy looked totally surprised as she turned red. Ross awkwardly stepped forward and did the same. We all knew we never did the "goodbye kiss thing." Ever. But I wanted an excuse to kiss Vicki.

"OK, then," Macy said stiffly with her hands at her side as she turned and stepped up on the trolley. Vicki followed. They walked toward some open seats at the front. The trolley conductor guy, a Black dude with a funny hat who was standing near the trolley steps and who was waiting for us and our episode to end, turned and gave me a wink. He then jumped aboard, hooking up the little chain at the top of the steps.

With a couple of rings of the trolley bell, they were off. We waved as they sped off up the hill.

With a big goofy smile on his face, Ross looked at me as if waiting for a well-deserved explanation.

"What?" I said.

"What the hell was that?" he said with a chuckle.

"What was *what?*" I said.

"*That,*" Ross said. "*That.*"

"Ah, I don't know what you mean, Maynard," I said.

Altogether it turned out to be a fantastic day. And now I had a date for the next night.

CHAPTER 10

DESPERATE TIMES LEAD TO DESPERATE MEASURES

My mouth was so dry I had trouble swallowing. It was still dark enough in the space I was in as to not be able to tell how big the area was. The ceiling, walls, and floor were a blackish dark grey coloration. It was impossible to know where the floor, ceiling, and walls joined—if, in fact, they did. It was as if I were suspended in space but the cold floor burned at my feet like a hot plate. There was an archway shape of light that I guessed to be about thirty feet away to my left. I hadn't noticed it earlier because it was slightly behind me. It had at some point brightened up and was now providing the little extra illumination in the room. I thought it could be a doorway of sorts. It was the only real source of light in the entire space.

Four of the little creatures were now three feet from me but had stopped from coming any closer. They had come together in a little group in front of me at the foot of the table. They stood there, totally expressionless, with their arms at their sides. Other than floating or gliding nearer to each other, they had yet to move in any way. They just stood there staring at me with those catfish eyes. The buzzard-looking things hadn't yet moved.

The table I woke up on with the sharp edges was directly between me and the light source that I took as a doorway. Even the table was hard to see, as it was black as well. Everything was dark. I found it odd that the table was higher than the alien's heads. Why would they have me up there and more importantly how did they get me up there? It made me look again at the buzzard statues.

I needed to make a break for that door. I needed to do it sooner than later, I thought to myself There's no way to clear the height of the table as it was about four and a half feet high Its sharp edges would mess me up again should I attempt to jump over it. The back of my leg was still bleeding from when I jumped off and ripped myself open.

In my head, I was quickly planning shit out. What I needed to do was bulldoze a couple of those little bastards over and bolt for that door. Where the door led I didn't know but it had to be better than standing there freezing in that stinky room with those creatures staring at me. I didn't know what their intentions were but I was sure they didn't invite me there for English lessons.

I didn't know how fast I could move. My body feels numb from the cold. If only I can stretch a bit. Get a feel for what I got going on.

OK. That was what I'd do. I'd just casually, slowly stretch and check myself out. I'm sure my little friends wouldn't mind. I'm sure they'd understand. A kid needed to stretch from time to time. Didn't he?

I slowly rotated my neck—first from right to left, then from left to right, while not allowing my eyes to leave the little brown beings. I made some gentle arm movements, lifting them out horizontally from my sides then opening and closing my fists. I ended the movement with my hands on my waist. The skin on my waist felt cold to my hands, which were now sweating and steaming. My efforts didn't seem to have any effect on the little martians. They didn't flinch. Feeling a little more comfortable in my strategy, I bent over slowly at the waist. I straightened back up slowly. *OK, all good there*, I thought to myself.

I slowly lifted my left leg, bending it at the knee. Then I put it back to the floor, leaving my biggest concern for last. My right knee had always been a problem. I have a touch of arthritis in that ol' boy and it had a habit of popping out of the joint. I lifted it slowly and, to my amazement, it felt great. When my upper thigh became horizontal to the floor, I started to lower it back down. It moved smoothly until it didn't. Suddenly, I felt pressure in the joint and it locked up solid. My foot was about nine inches off the floor. It had done this before. I knew all I had to do was push a steady pressure and it would push past the problem area but my balance wasn't what it used to be, so I very slowly moved my left hand to rest my fingers on the table at my side. When I had a bit of a perch on the table, I took a breath and counted to three. I pushed a firm, steady pressure and my knee began to move. As it moved through the locked-up position, it decided to let out a loud snap, then my foot hit the floor with a thud.

In a split second, the buzzard-like creatures lit up as if hit by a spotlight from above. Now I could see them more clearly. They looked super imposing. The head looked like a big black bird's head with large black eyes and a black beak-looking thing. They looked like they were made of obsidian. Everything was fricken black. But the eyes were like glass and reflected light like mirrors. The body was long and tubular and went all the way down to the darkness as if it took up root in the floor.

The things looked mechanical. Completely void of life or emotion. They had what I'm guessing were arms, which looked sort of like tree branches that shot straight up motionless and disappeared into the darkness.

I almost shit myself.

I removed my hand from the table and put some weight on my knee. My knee once again snapped. The buzzard's head moved forward on its long, saggy neck. Their black eyes peered at me intensely.

These things seemed to be reacting to sound more than movement. I needed to be careful.

I turned my head slowly, looking down toward my injured leg and noticed the little brown fuck that had been behind me was now in a crouched position and had moved its face within four inches of my wound and its tongue was out and lightly licking at the blood that was running down my leg. It startled the shit out of me. I jumped and screamed.

Without even thinking, I swatted the little prick away, sending him flying backward into the dark. Within a second, one of the buzzards closed the distance between him and me. The little aliens that were at the end of the table also went flying, pushed out of the way by the big black creature. One alien was caught between the table and the buzzard's massive body. It let out a shriek and fell to the floor. The buzzard's arms were wrapped around me. The arms weren't at all like tree branches but were more like octopus arms. I could feel the pressure and suction of its suction cups. The suction was so intense, every cup caused immense pain, sucking blood to the surface of my skin. I was under full assault. I again screamed out. Before I could catch my breath, I was lifted high into the black air and slammed down on the granite table, face first. This removed the skin on my chin and knees. I fought to roll over against the force of the suction cups. I felt my skin rip and tear away from some of the cups. I managed to roll to my back with my legs facing the buzzard.

I pulled back and cocked my legs with my knee popping and cracking. I thrusted forward with my heels with all my might, striking the buzzard somewhere along its body, which was now pressed up tight to the foot of the table. The buzzard never moved. It was like kicking a schoolbus, so I was propelled backwards from my own force off the table and hit the floor on the other side with a thud. Now I had a clear shot at the doorway.

Without even thinking about what I was doing, I up and shot toward the light at that door. It took me less than four seconds to cover the distance. The doorway was only about four feet high and I was in such a mad sprint that I had no choice but to dive through it on the run.

On the other side, there was slightly more light. I had been in the darkness for so long the light caused my eyes to burn. As I stood up, I saw that my knees left bloody skid marks on the floor. It appeared I was in a long, tubular hallway or corridor that had black circular shapes on the left along its length. I'm guessing they were windows or portholes to the outside. The walls along both sides and floor surface were covered in these nodules. I took them as rivets and the ones on the floor hurt my foot when I stepped on one. Along the ceiling were hoses and piping that ran the length of the hall. The ceiling was low and my hair rubbed and sometimes got caught in things. My hair getting pulled irritated me tremendously. I stood with my legs slightly bent.

I glanced back. My heart was pounding. Nothing appeared through the blackness of the doorway, but I wasn't waiting around till something did. If it was any consolation to my psyche, there was no way the buzzards could fit through that opening.

I turned and eased down the corridor in the opposite direction. The hall was littered with garbage and junk. There were other indented arches in the wall along the right side of the hallway, which I took to be other doorways that were closed. Along the length of this hall between the floor and the vertical wall on the right was a trough of sorts. I wasn't sure what purpose it would serve. At the far end of this corridor appeared an opening.

I hurried clumsily along with my beat-up body. I moved as if I were walking on a moving train. My balance was messed up. As I forged forward, my foot kicked something, sending it flying down the hall in the direction I was heading. I raced over to see what I had kicked. I bent over and picked it up in the poor light. It was a woman's handbag. A blue handbag. It looked strangely familiar somehow to my confused state of mind. I looked inside and saw a lady's wallet, a blue Bic lighter, and an empty pack of Newport smokes. I stared blankly getting lost in the bag. When everything started to register, I became so horrified that my fingers were unable to hang onto the bag. I dropped it to the floor. I couldn't breathe. I couldn't wrap my head around what was happening. I backed away from the bag as I stared at it lying there on the floor. My foot stepped into the trough and I rolled my ankle. It sent me flying, smashing my head on the wall and jarring me from my vapor-locked brain. I fell to the floor, holding my twisted ankle in one hand and my cracked cranium in the other. I rolled up in a ball, yelling in pain and frustration. I put my hand over my mouth and, with my eyes wide open, peered over at the black door I had come through. I got a grip of myself, stood up again, and ran to and through the opening.

I was at an intersection of sorts. There was another hall that went perpendicular left and right. Looking back, nothing came through the black doorway about fifty feet in the distance. I stared at the blue bag lying on the floor, about twenty feet back in the middle of the hall. As sweat, tears, and snot ran down my face, I walked off to the left with my hand just touching the wall.

I slowly started getting my wits back about me. It struck me as odd that, although there was obvious illumination around me, I couldn't figure out how the light was being generated. There were no actual light sources. No one thing was giving off light. Things just had their own slight illumination of various levels. But at least I could now make out everything before me. I remembered Ross reading me something from one of his nerdy books that explained a theory about how ionizing radiation could be used to produce light. Then I thought, *Holy shit, radiation. Ross, you asshole, thanks a lot, wait till I see you.*

Even in my ongoing state of self-turmoil, I was cold. Although my skin felt moist as if I were sweating I was still shivering. The bottom of my feet felt burnt from frostbite. My eyes scanned the items on the floor for something I could wrap around me or wear. A lot of this crap was clothing. Pants, shirts, jackets, hats. There were shoes everywhere, but it seemed no two matched. I searched intensely to find a couple of shoes that would fit my size eleven feet.

I found a backpack. I scooped a handful of garbage together to build a mat so I didn't have to kneel on the ice-cold floor. My skinned knees were a sore, scabby mess. The backpack had a pair of hiking boots with the laces knotted together at the ends then half hitched around the pack's shoulder strap. I untied the knots, pulled slack into the laces, and looked inside for a size. Oh my God. "Size eleven" was stamped on the insole. I quickly unzipped the large section of the pack and rummaged through the contents. The first thing I saw was an unopened bottle of water. I spun off the lid and guzzled half of it down in one gulp, spun the lid back on, and placed it on the floor beside me. I pulled out a red hoody. *This will fit you, Maynard,* I thought to myself. I pulled it on and zipped it up. The zipper was so cold it sent a shiver through my body as it touched my bare skin.

Next, there was a pair of woollen socks that had obviously been worn as they were stiff and crusty. I happily pulled them on my feet. I quickly looked into one of the smaller side pockets. I found a park entry receipt that read, "Mir Woods, one adult, twelve dollars." The date stamp on it in a smudged purple color said, "1:30 pm, May 12, 2018." "That was fifteen months ago," I whispered to myself. I balled it up in my hand and threw it on the floor.

I grabbed the remains of the water, threw it in the pack, stood up, zipped the big compartment closed, and swung the pack on over my shoulders.

I looked at the boots. *I better find some pants first*, I thought. My feet were already feeling a whole lot better standing on my little island of discarded clothes. I could see a large pair of men's Carhartt pants over along the wall lying in the trough. I thought, *I hope they are not wet*. I hurried over and grabbed them. They were already unzipped and dry, so I quickly pulled them on, being careful not to catch anything in the zipper. Resuming my position on the floor, I pulled on and laced up the boots. I jumped to my feet. "Perfect! Shocola," I declared as I pretended to get weak-legged. I chuckled for a second at my own silliness. Then reality came back to me.

OK. Now to find my way out of here.

The lighting in these tubular corridors was again slowly becoming poor. About halfway down the next hall, I stopped for a moment to see if I could see anything out of one of the windows that still lined the left. The portholes were about forty-eight inches from the floor, obviously constructed for someone or something vertically challenged. I reluctantly pressed my face to the glassy material. Looking down, I could see the lights of the Bay Bridge in the darkness and the headlights of traffic as it crossed the bridge from San Fran to Oakland and back. "Holy shit, I'm in an aircraft," I said out loud. It was night in the city and I was obviously very high up—I suspected several hundred feet. It didn't dawn on me at the time but if I were in an aircraft, how was I supposed to get to safety?

The glass froze my face and my chin left blood on the glass. I stood there for a second staring as a drop of blood froze to the window. It struck me that the stench in the air had become much stronger and I swore that, oddly, I could smell cigarette smoke. Again I thought of Vicki.

I pushed myself farther and as I got to the far end of the corridor, it made a corner and took off to the right. It became another hallway that had a room off it to the right about twenty feet up. There was a ruckus coming from that room. The room was slightly more brightly lit than the hall so I could see shadow movements being cast from inside the room onto the floor in the hall there ahead of me.

I turned the corner and inched toward the room. My heart started to pound again. My mouth was so dry. I rubbed my tongue vigorously on my teeth, trying to stimulate the creation of spit. I thought of that remaining mouthful of water I had in the backpack.

I inched so quietly toward the room. The smell was repulsive. I could hear a droning of machinery. Thumping and swishing sounds. I got to the edge of the door. I was hesitant to look in, but if I needed to get past this door, I had to see if it was safe to cross the plain of the open doorway without being seen. The hall ahead of me was dark, but at this point, there was nowhere left to go but forward into that darkness. The reflection of shadows from the room now moved at my feet. I told myself I could do this. I took a deep breath and spun toward the wall. The toe of my boot made contact with a thud. I looked up in disappointment, mouthing the word, "fuck." I rested my forehead on the cold wall and closed my eyes as I searched myself for courage. I could hear my breath reflected on the wall directly back into my ears. My fingertips just hovered over the cold surface in front of me. The doorway was now just to the left of my face.

"OK, I'll do this. On three."

"One, two . . .

Before I finished my carefully planned procedure, I peered around the edge of the door into the room.

In the semi-lit room, there were two of the little freaks. They stood with their backs to me, facing some moving equipment ahead of them. One stood back several steps, motionless, with its arms hanging at its side. A cloud of smoke seemed to hang around its head. The second guy was positioned ahead of the first and appeared to be wearing gloves on his hands. I could see some type of strapping come around the back of both their big heads.

The forward-positioned alien's skinny, sinewy arms were working vigorously, operating what I guessed was a remote-control device that was connected to a cable. This was the first time I'd seen one of these creatures move. It was weird, man.

The floor appeared to be a metal grating that was different than what I was standing on. It was suspended somehow from the darkness below. The whole area was littered with clothing and garbage.

The equipment gave off a hum and I could hear noise coming from below the floor. With a pop, I could see movement as something came into view from out of the darkness. When I realized what it was I looked at the blood rushed out of my head and I felt like I was going to pass out. There were people somehow suspended upside down by their legs from the darkness above and were moving in the direction of a metal device. I could see six people. It was as if I was looking into a butcher shop cooler. They were naked and motionless with their arms hanging freely below them. One of the victims was small like a child. My God. *I thought they were dead*, I thought in a panic.

The alien seemed to manipulate the bodies into position over a conveyor chain. The little monster operating the remote looked up in that direction as its hands operated the remote control. The alien that seemed to be supervising the operation just stood there with puffs of smoke coming out of its head.

I watched in horror as the bodies swung into position and fell onto the chain. The chain moved the bodies along as robotic prods shot in from the sides and roughly manipulated the bodies into a face-up, head-first position on the chain. The conveyor chain fed into a metal machine that looked like an industrial toaster. Cracking and sucking sounds came out from the machine. I felt my stomach turning. I felt myself heating up. I felt anger well up inside me. I wanted to kill those little bastards. I did my best to stay quiet.

Almost as fast as the bodies were fed into the machine, a conveyer chain coming out the other side carried the bodies out at a lower level. The bodies looked the same as they did as they entered the machine, but I could see a definite puncture wound near the lower abdomen. The body was a yellow greyish color. Those poor people. When the little one came out of the device I couldn't bring myself to look any longer. The conveyer carried them along several feet then dumped them through an opening in the wall.

What was all this about?

Why were these creatures killing us? What was the purpose of this machine? In all the movies I'd ever seen, people were abducted for scientific tests. Not blatant butchery.

Suddenly, I gagged and coughed and threw my hand to my mouth. The aliens both swung around. The supervisor alien had a smoking cigarette jammed into one of the holes I thought were nostrils. The cherry at the end of the smoke was flashing orange as he puffed away. I could see his catfish eyes peer at me through a set of goggles. He somehow looked extremely pissed.

Our eyes met. I panicked and, without a thought, bolted across the door opening and ran into the darkness of the hallway ahead. In the darkness, I hit a wall at the end of the hall and fell to the floor, slightly stunned. I quickly stood back up and peered back toward the room of horrors. The dirty little bastards were standing there looking at me, motionless, through their goggles. Two other of the things were there now as well, standing at the hallway intersection farther back with their little arms to their sides, assuming their usual stance. I put my hands to my face to rub my eyes and leaned against the freezing wall with my left shoulder. Suddenly, the wall gave way as if it had vanished and I fell into another semi-dark room.

As my ears passed what should have been the plane of the wall, my eardrums popped and my arms flung out to grasp what was no longer there. I fell to the floor hard-knocking my wind out. Quickly looking back, I saw the wall opening heal closed behind me. I was in another dark, cold area, and starting to slip. The stench was unbearable. The floor was at a steep sloping angle off toward the craft's outer wall and now I was sliding toward that wall. I did my best to keep from sliding, but there was nothing to hang onto.

The angle was too steep and slippery. There was a jelly type material on the floor that gave off a pungent acidic sour smell. There was a large translucent area on the wall that was allowing moonlight from outside to beam in. It was a large exterior hatch with a translucent plate. . . . Looking back up toward where I fell through the wall, I could see some dim light coming from a rectangular opening where the conveyer chain was dumping bodies into this space from the other side.

I slid down until I hit a pile of something at the bottom along the wall and came to a stop with my face to the floor. My now hot, sweaty body was steaming in the cold. There were other sources causing steam, as well. With my face lying pressed on the slimy floor, I lifted my head and slowly opened my eyes again. With the dim light being allowed in by the translucent area several feet from me, I could see the silhouette of an outstretched arm and a hand that seemed to be forever frozen, grasping for the heavens. I reached up and, with my free hand, scraped a cupped hand full of slime off my face. I turned my head to further survey my situation. Directly in front of my face were two familiar ocean-blue eyes. I could make out freckles and red hair in the dim light. As my brain struggled to understand, I panicked and screamed. I choked as I inhaled some of the slime. My mind wanted to shut down. I could feel myself losing consciousness as I struggled to find oxygen. Suddenly, the big hatch began to swing open. I felt a tremendous suction as air rushed over me. My ears again popped as I blacked out.

What Beau didn't realize at the time, nor would ever learn, was that the victims of these abductions were euthanized in the theater where Beau had first regained consciousness. While the people were still unconscious from the anesthetic, the aliens had used during the abduction process, the aliens would perform exploratory tests on the bodies. These tests could last for up to forty minutes. When they were content, they would end the humans' lives by dripping a chemical in their nostrils. It was that simple and uneventful. The heart would experience complete paralysis immediately and it would be all over.

The aliens had learned from experience over the years of harvesting people that it was far less of a problem to make them dead as quickly as possible. Having a human wake up in the theater had proven to be a major issue in the past. Beau was proving to be a perfect example of this—wandering the corridors of the ship unabated.

It was uncertain why the anesthetic wore off Beau prematurely.

When the aliens' victims were done within the theater, they were transported to an area in the ship where they were collected for the final process. This final process was the reason the aliens were harvesting humans in the first place.

Very little has ever been discussed about the anatomy and biological functions of an alien. One thing for certain is that all living things, and it doesn't matter where they originate, require a source of fuel for energy. The aliens were naturally no different. Now before we all lose our minds thinking that ET was chowing down on old Uncle Tom like a cheeseburger, let's actually see what was going down.

When they entered the atmosphere of earth centuries ago, it quickly became apparent that they would need to adjust to find a different source of energy. They found that a large variety of vegetation everywhere was adequate to supply the sugars and proteins they required and that chlorophyll was beneficial to the process. The problem was that their endocrine systems were never designed to facilitate digestion. What they managed to learn fast through necessity was that, with the addition of bile into their feeding process, the food source would quickly and thoroughly be converted into energy. The problem was solved.

The aliens had this process down to a science and, after over the years, had been managing to thrive in earth's system. They found that cows were one of the best sources of bile as cows have four stomachs and produce a tremendous amount of bile. Cows are also herbivores and the cow's bile has specialized bile properties that were also extremely beneficial. When harvesting the bile from cattle, the process was completed in the field as the animals were too large to bring to the ship. Various tests, if any, were carried out on the spot. The remains of their bovine victims have been an area of extreme interest and concern to humans for years. In areas where the aliens were operating that didn't have a large easy cattle supply, humans were always the quick go-to for them.

Now, the process of extracting bile from humans is relatively easy. It could be carried out in the original abduction theater on the ship, but the aliens had devised a robotic device that helped them deal with the weight of their victims and collecting the bile product. They had put together a small area on the ship where the whole process could be carried out and the bodies could be stored until attended to. They set up the area near where the ship was equipped with an external hatch so they could jettison the remains when they were done with them.

CHAPTER 11

A DREAM SEQUENCE

I could feel the warmth of the sun. A bright yellowness appeared through my eyelids. I opened my eyes to see the brightness of God's glorious light. I could hear children laughing. I could smell the ocean and burgers. I could hear a dog barking as he played happily with his family. I could hear the music of Hubert Emerson coming from somewhere along Fisherman's Wharf.

"Hey, Beau! Beauy! Hey, Beau!" I looked down off my perch from the tenth row of the beach bleachers, across the sand to the water's edge, where Vicki was waving and trying to get my attention. She was trying to push a small rowboat off the sand into the water. I waved and she waved back to summon me over. A little nudge and a voice from my right said, "Hey, man. I think your presence is being required." I looked to my right to see a smiling Ross with Macy sitting at his side.

"I think maybe you're right," I said.

"Can you come and help me go boating?" she called.

"Sure thing, Vicki." I ran down from the bleachers and happily skipped across the beach. "Jump in, Vicki, and I'll push us out," I instructed. She scurried off to the front of the boat and took a seat on the front rung. With a little push, the boat began to float and with another little shove, the boat took off and I jumped in.

I couldn't believe I was in a boat. On the water. I grabbed the oars and started us out toward the wave-breaker wall. I don't ever remember the sky and the ocean looking so blue. It was a glorious day and I was remarkably happy there on the water with Vicki. I looked back to see Macy and Ross waving to us from the bleachers. We waved back. I looked back at Vicki, and her beautiful, smiling face. Her tanned skin, her freckles, her red hair blowing in the gentle west-coast trade winds. But best of all were those ocean-blue eyes. We stared at each other from across the little boat, looking deep into each other's thoughts. I told Vicki that I loved her. The words just came out.

"What did you say, silly?" Vicki replied.

"I said I lo—"

Suddenly, there was a tremendous impact on the bottom of the little wooden boat. I dropped the oars. Vicki shrieked as we both grabbed the boat's edge and hung on. Our smiles immediately turned into fear. Then without warning, my side of the boat was thrust into the air. The oars turned on their moorings and spun down toward Vicki. Other items that were in the boat fell toward her, hitting her as her side of the boat took a nosedive into the water.

I could see Vicki below me with a bloody lip as an oar struck her. She hung on tightly as she sank into the water. She looked up at me with fear and confusion.

Unable to hang on any longer, I plunged into the water. Everything turned black.

CHAPTER 12

TAKING OUT THE TRASH

I struck the water hard. I mean *hard*. As if I had fallen from a substantial height. I may have even injured myself, but was too dazed to know for sure.

Am I in the ocean? How did I get in the fricken ocean? I thought, while trying to comprehend what was happening.

The water was freezing cold. I shivered uncontrollably, my teeth chattering as the coldness stunned me back to consciousness. As my face broke the surface, I opened my eyes while gasping for air. It was the dead of night. The stars and moon were out. Directly above me in the sky was a large circular area of blackness, as if something were between myself and the stars. Around the perimeter of the blackness, the regular pattern of random stars reappeared. I had trouble getting a good look as the area was directly overhead and my neck was too messed up to hold the position required to see. The saltwater burned at my open wounds.

Then without any notice or sound out of the corner of my eye, I watched as the strange black hole shot off and vanished into the sky to the northeast. The stars opened up above me.

I could tell by the reflection of the moon on the water that other objects were floating in the water all around. My hands and arms ran into things as I struggled to tread water. I could now see the Bay Bridge lights just off to the south and, in the distance, the lights of Alcatraz farther off to the northwest.

As my eyes adjusted to the light—or lack thereof—I began to notice movement in the water around me. Other than my own gasps and struggles, it was quiet, but I could hear splashing around me and the tires of cars crossing the Bay Bridge in the distance.

I became fixated on the flesh-colored masses and the trash floating around me and watched in disbelief as the masses were systematically jerked below the surface of the water. Dorsal fins were beginning to break the surface all around. I began to further panic as I felt something strike my foot in the darkness.

Not this again, I thought to myself.

I knew I was in big trouble.

The multiple injuries. The long period without food. The shortage of fluids to drink. The cold, the hypothermia. The intensive periods of fear and confusion.

My brain started to misfire with a random collage of information.

I pictured aliens standing around smoking cigarettes. I saw Ross bring the Vega home for the first time. I saw my mom arguing with my dad about Christmas. The stars spun out of control overhead.

I saw Macy doing the chocolate dance and sitting at her desk at work. Voices were saying, "Pull up beside him, pull up beside him." Vicki asked where we should go for coffee. I saw flashes of spotlights upon me. I saw Vicki and me standing at the Alcatraz sign at Fisherman's Wharf. *I'll grab him. Grab the hoody. Branding doesn't hurt the cows, Beau. Nothing good ever come out of the water. Get him in the boat.* An intermittent view of the Bay Bridge spun out of control before my eyes. Risotto. Sharks. Newport's. Gargoyles. Oyster Rockefeller.

I felt it grab me. Tear at me. Thrust me out of the water. I screamed, swallowing gulps of saltwater. My arms flailed in a battle for my life. I had nothing left. Everything went ice cold. All went black. My brain turned off.

"You're OK, son. You're OK. You're safe. You're in our boat and you're safe. Can you hear me?

"Grab that blanket under the seat, Chip, please. I think there is still hot coffee in the Thermos there also."

Muffled words started to come together. I could feel something solid under me. There was light. I again opened my eyes. It took me a second to focus. Some kind of foggy greenish color stood over me. I firmly grabbed the green with two clenched fists. As my eyes focused, the face of an older man leaned over me in a green lumber jacket. The man looked concerned, then shot down a warm, friendly smile. "You're OK, son," said the friendly face. "What's your name, son? Do you know your name?"

"Beau, sir. My name is Beau," I said through clenched teeth.

"Well, Beau, you're the biggest fish we've pulled out of the water this week. Don't know if you'll be good eating though. Seems those sharks may disagree," the man said, smiling.

"Nothing good ever came from the ocean, sir," I muttered.

The old man lost his smile. "Let's get this kid to shore, Chip."

CHAPTER 13

THEY'RE NOT GOING TO BELIEVE THIS SHIT

Joel was standing around the base of the water tower on Alcatraz. It was a quarter after midnight, Sunday morning. He had decided to get an extra night shift in before this pay period ended.

It was a particularly quiet night on the Rock as there were no repairs or crews scheduled. The four security fellows were pretty much the sole occupants on the island this night.

The security detail had a small office set up just in the main building around the corner from the store.

The fellas took their turn doing the rounds while one of the guys always stayed back to man the office and monitor the radios.

It was protocol to have three men head out in three different directions at the same time and be back at the office at a predetermined time. It generally took fifteen minutes to make the sweep. The radios were usually a chatterbox at that time.

It was a casual operation on the night shift as no one particular guy ever considered himself the supervisor. All the fellas got along well and were all over sixty years of age. The Alcatraz full-time staff called them "the Crusty Crew." They were kind of known for their use of colorful language and a "I-don't-give-a-shit" attitude.

In between the surveillance rounds, a lot of hours were spent playing crib and cards. Far more cribs and cards than rounds of surveillance, if you can imagine.

They used radios to keep in communication with each other at all times. It was policy as Alcatraz could be a dangerous place to walk around at night, not to mention that only lights deemed "essential" were allowed to be left on. If a guy wasn't extra careful, he could inadvertently walk right off the edge of a cliff and end up floating in the bay with the sharks. This is why the park service used the same guys over and over from a pool of twelve security personnel. They knew the lay of the land and knew how to stay out of trouble.

Certain lights were allowed to be turned on along the trail that encircled the island. They referred to this path as the perimeter trail. The perimeter trail was paved and had handrails for the most part. Particularly on the ocean side. The lighting was not great along the perimeter trail, but the guys weren't allowed to leave the main building without a flashlight. If any of the fellas encountered any trouble or questionable activity, they were under strict orders to stay put and radio in immediately. Two of the others would immediately be sent over that way. There were plenty of areas around Alcatraz that were so sketchy they were even out of bounds for the security boys.

"How long has Joel been gone?" old Wilf asked as he stared into a hand of cards.

"Hell, I don't know," another said, lazily looking at his watch.

"Maybe you should give him a call on the radio," Wilf said, looking at the fella sitting behind the desk.

"Yeah, a lot of fucking good that's gonna do," he said and pointed with his lips at a radio lying on the chair where Joel had been sitting.

The three crusty old farts broke out chuckling.

"Where did he go anyway?" one of the guys, Todd, asked.

"I think he said he was going for a smoke," said the fella at the desk. "I don't know. I wasn't paying any attention."

The three men broke out into chuckles again.

"Well, maybe one of us should head out and check on him."

"Aw, I'll go," Todd said as he stood up and stretched. "I gotta go for a piss anyway."

"Well, take your radio. Oh, and bring your flashlight, for Christ's sake, so you don't fall into the fucking ocean." The room once again broke out into laughter.

Joel stood in the dark, motionless, with his eyes transfixed in the sky toward the Bay Bridge. His mouth was open and there was a cigarette hanging, stuck to his bottom lip, supporting a long ash finger. His eyes didn't blink as his left thumb inadvertently flicked the lighter he was holding.

From Alcatraz, the Bay Bridge can be seen to the southeast, connecting San Francisco to Oakland. The Bay Bridge is a behemoth of a structure with ten lanes and two layers of traffic that span four miles in length. The upper towers of the bridge are more than 526 feet high. The bridge is a suspension bridge. The mighty cables that span the towers are adorned with lights to ensure aircraft stay clear. That bridge is loud and proud and at night it's visible for tens of miles, not to mention it's very beautiful, although the Golden Gate Bridge gets all the attention.

"Holy fuck. There you are," a voice broke the silence.

"Jesus H Christ!" Joel yelled as his smoke fell to the ground, sending sparks flying everywhere.

"What are you trying to do—scare the living shit out of me?"

"Fuck sakes," he said, patting at his front, thinking that the cherry had fallen off his smoke into his shirt.

"What are you doing out here pulling on yer pecker?" Todd asked, chuckling.

"Fuck! Did you see that?" Joel asked, turning back toward the bridge, clearly shaken.

"No. See *what?*"

"There was a big blackness in the sky over there by the bridge," Joel said in a panicked voice.

"Ah, it's midnight, Joel," said Todd. "The whole fucking sky is black."

"No, man, I mean, like, all the stars were blacked out as this big black mass moved in from over Oakland. I watched it. I saw it come in. Then it dropped down just below the bridge lights. A big section of the fucking bridge went black for a second. Then it raised back up, hovered for a second, then fucked off over the bridge to the south."

Todd had never seen Old Joel shaken up like this before.

"Hey, man, take it easy, old boy. You're starting to scare me," said Todd. "Yer gonna give yourself and me a heart attack."

"No man, I'm OK. I mean, you see where that boat is out there in the water? It was just over there."

Todd looked over, squinting to see something there he could agree with.

Joel finally turned to look at Todd. He reached up, lifting his cap with his left hand, and scratched his head with the right and started to chuckle. Todd noticed a big smile develop on Joel's face under his big floor-broom moustache. "They're not going to believe this one, Todd."

"Let's get back to the guys," Todd said. "They're going to start worrying about us."

Joel put his hands on Todd's shoulders and turned him around toward the security office. Then he put his arm up across Todd's back and started to steer and hurry Todd back to the office as he jabbered away in Todd's ear.

Joel could be heard repeating, "They're not going to believe this. They're just not going to believe this one."

End.

CONCLUSION

Bill and Chip Wheeler were adamant about what they had witnessed in the Bay that night and their story would later be substantiated by what Joel Reber witnessed from his view on the Rock.

Beau survived his ordeal. He never shared his experience with anyone, particularly not the authorities, and he fully denied the circulating stories of how he ended up in the waters of the Bay.

A full investigation into the disappearance of Vicki Doss was conducted and, although Beau was the last to be seen with her, there was never any evidence that Beau was involved in her disappearance and he was ultimately cleared of any involvement.

In the end, Vicki was added to the long list of people who had gone missing in the Bay area.

Twenty-one that year alone.

Bill and Chip still fish together, although they no longer fish at night. They changed the area they fish and have stopped being harassed by sharks.

Beau went on to get his degree in electrical engineering and resumed his career at the UOSF alongside his friends Ross and Macy.

He never again spoke of what happened.

SPECIAL THANKS

Firstly, I'd like to thank my Grandma Piquette, who was responsible for getting my brother and me reading at a young age and for being a devoted purveyor of five-cent comic books.

Secondly, I need to sincerely thank my darling wife, Tammi, for her support and for helping me save my transcript when TextEdit got a virus, turning my work into a dog's lunch.

I also need to thank Lee Schmidt for pre-pre-editing my atrocious grammar, spelling, and punctuation.

Thanks to Hannah Nott for her amazing illustrative skills. Please check her out at #fromconcept2art.com

And special thanks to my editor and publishers at FriesenPress.

Without these people, I couldn't have managed.

RICHARD A. PIQUETTE

Author

Lightning Source UK Ltd.
Milton Keynes UK
UKHW012023050922
408363UK00001B/199